D1053196

LIVING WITH VAMPIRES

BY JEREMY STRONG

ILLUSTRATED BY SCOULAR ANDERSON

Librarian Reviewer
Kathleen Baxter
Children's Literature Consultant
formerly with Anoka County Library, MN
BA College of Saint Catherine, St. Paul, MN
MA in Library Science, University of Minnesota

Reading Consultant
Elizabeth Stedem
Educator/Consultant, Colorado Springs, CO
MA in Elementary Education, University of Denver, CO

STONE ARCH BOOKS
Minneapolis   San Diego

First published in the United States in 2007
by Stone Arch Books,
151 Good Counsel Drive, P.O. Box 669,
Mankato, Minnesota 56002.
www.stonearchbooks.com

Published by arrangement with
Barrington Stoke Ltd, Edinburgh.

Library of Congress Cataloging-in-Publication Data
Strong, Jeremy.
    Living with Vampires / by Jeremy Strong; illustrated by Scoular
Anderson.
        p. cm. — (Pathway Books)
    Summary: In order to have an opportunity to spend time with the
heavenly Miranda at a school dance, Kevin Vlad will have to let his vampire
parents help chaperone, but how will he keep them from turning everyone
into zombies?
    ISBN-13: 978-1-59889-104-1 (hardcover)
    ISBN-10: 1-59889-104-9 (hardcover)
    ISBN-13: 978-1-59889-261-1 (paperback)
    ISBN-10: 1-59889-261-4 (paperback)
    [1. Vampires—Fiction. 2. Schools—Fiction. 3. Parents—Fiction.]
I. Anderson, Scoular, ill. II. Title. III. Series.
PZ7.S92356Liv 2007
[Fic]—dc22   2006007176

Art Director: Heather Kindseth
Cover Illustrator: Brett Hawkins
Graphic Designer: Kay Fraser

1 2 3 4 5 6 11 10 09 08 07 06

TABLE OF CONTENTS

CHAPTER 1

NO ESCAPE

Kevin Vladd was not looking forward to Tuesday evening. His parents, Mr. and Mrs. Vladd, were not looking forward to Tuesday evening, either.

And his teacher, Mrs. Fottle, was definitely not looking forward to Tuesday evening.

Tuesday was the day of the parent-teacher conferences. There was no way to escape!

Kevin did not like those meetings.

< 5 >

Kevin liked his teacher, Mrs. Fottle. But he never knew what she was going to say next to his parents.

He tried to do well at school. It was just that he had better things to do. He would sit and stare out of the window for hours looking at the clouds.

If there weren't any clouds to gaze at, he could always stare at Miranda.

Miranda had long, black hair. Miranda had lovely, dark eyes. Miranda looked like a princess.

Kevin thought Miranda was heaven on legs.

The problem was that every other boy in the school thought Miranda was heaven on legs, too.

< 6 >

< 7 >

Grant did, more than anyone. Kevin did not like Grant.

But now that Tuesday had come, Kevin had other things to think about.

Kevin and his parents were waiting outside the classroom for Mrs. Fottle to finish talking to Grant and his mom. What will Mrs. Fottle say about me? Kevin wondered. He hoped it would be something nice.

Kevin liked Mrs. Fottle. Most of the time she was kind and helpful and said nice things about him.

That's most of the time.

Kevin's mom and dad hadn't met Mrs. Fottle before. He hoped that it would all go well.

< 8 >

< 9 >

He knew his parents didn't have any dinner before they came to the conference. Kevin did not like to think what they might do if they were hungry. But there was nothing he could do about it.

The classroom door opened, and his enemy, Grant, and his mom came out. Grant stuck out his tongue. Kevin looked away. He followed his parents into the classroom.

"Kevin's math has improved," Mrs. Fottle began, "but I have to tell you that I think he has a problem."

Kevin sat up. What had he done? Had Mrs. Fottle seen him flicking paper balls at Grant? Or staring at Miranda in class?

< 10 >

Kevin's dad inched a little closer to Mrs. Fottle. Too close, Kevin thought.

"What is the problem?" Kevin's dad asked the teacher.

Mrs. Fottle opened a folder of work.

< 11 >

"I asked everyone to draw a picture of their dad or mom," she said. "And Kevin drew this. There's an awful lot of blood in it, don't you think?"

She held up the picture, and Kevin's parents looked at it. He had drawn his father with Dracula fangs. Blood was dripping from them.

Kevin's mom clapped her hands and smiled at her husband. "Darling, it looks just like you!"

Mrs. Fottle did not think it was funny. She began to huff and puff. "This is not a joke. This drawing is very upsetting. You should know, Kevin has handed in other pictures like this."

Mrs. Fottle pulled out some more pictures that Kevin had done.

< 12 >

< 13 >

"Look at this one. Zombies! And this one. Vampires! I really think Kevin should see a counselor. There must be awful things going on in his head," said Mrs. Fottle.

Kevin's dad smiled. "The thing is, Mrs. Fottle, it's not in his head." He lifted back his upper lip and showed her his teeth.

Mrs. Fottle took one look at the sharp, white fangs and went very pale. "Oh," she said, softly. "Oh, dear! I think I'm going to faint."

And she did. She fell forward across her desk.

Kevin's mom clapped her hands. "Supper!" she cried. "I'm starving!"

Kevin's parents sank their teeth into Mrs. Fottle's neck.

< 14 >

Kevin's parents were Grade Three Vampires. No wonder Kevin was having these problems.

< 15 >

< 16 >

CHAPTER 2

ALL YOU NEED TO KNOW ABOUT VAMPIRES

There are four kinds of vampires.

Grade One Vampires are the scariest. They only come out at night. They rest in their coffins during the day. These are the ones you often see in films or read about in books. They have white faces and fangs that drip blood. They can turn into bats and fly. They suck blood and leave lots of bodies around, which is very messy.

< 17 >

Grade Two Vampires have less power. They can also turn into bats. They leave lots of dead bodies around, too. Like Grade Ones, Grade Two vamps only come out at night, but they don't have coffins. They just hang out all day in damp, dark caves, getting wet and muddy.

Grade Three Vampires can go out in daylight. They suck people's blood, but they can't kill anyone. Their victims just faint, and when they wake up, they can't remember what happened to them.

Grade Three Vampires can turn people into zombies, but even that wears off after a while. They live in houses and sleep in beds, which is very smart of them.

< 18 >

Grade Four Vampires are hopeless.

They can't even suck blood. They just lick your skin, which is revolting. All the other vampires agree that Grade Fours are nothing but a big joke.

To Kevin, none of this was a joke. If your parents are vampires, it's not funny at all.

Even if they're only Grade Three.

Kevin was unlucky in another way. He was the only one in his family who wasn't a vampire.

Every hundred years, a vampire family has one child who is not a vampire. Kevin was that child.

What Kevin wanted more than anything was to have normal parents.

< 19 >

He wanted to be able to go out with them and know they wouldn't sink their fangs into someone's neck.

Most of all he wanted to go to the school dance. He wanted to dance with Miranda, the most beautiful girl in the school.

The problem was that the dance was for teachers, students, and their parents. If Kevin went to the dance, his parents would have to go, too. That could only mean more trouble.

Kevin didn't know if he was ever going to tell them about this one. How could he take a pair of vampires to a dance? Anything could happen. Kevin sighed sadly.

< 20 >

His parents had finished their meal and were wiping the blood from their fangs with some paper tissues.

Mrs. Vladd smiled at her son. "Mrs. Fottle said that your math is much, much better."

"Mom, I don't care about my math," said Kevin. "Will Mrs. Fottle be okay?"

"Oh, she'll be fine. When she wakes up she won't remember a thing. Now what's all this about a school dance?"

Kevin's mom had seen the big poster on the classroom wall. "You haven't said a thing about it. I thought you liked dances. Are we all going?" she asked.

Kevin gave another sigh. His parents often made him sigh.

< 21 >

CHAPTER 3

HOW TO CURE
A VAMPIRE

After the parent-teacher conferences, Mrs. Fottle had to take three days off from work. She said she felt worn out. She didn't remember what had happened. But it was all too much for Kevin.

Things couldn't go on like this. The shame was too much for him. And it was scary. He kept worrying that his friends would find out his secret.

< 22 >

The date of the school dance was coming up. He really wanted to go. But if he went, his parents would go, too. Miranda would be there. How could he put her in such danger?

Kevin knew that somehow he would have to stop his parents from being vampires. He had five days to figure out how to do it.

Kevin sat in his bedroom and thought and thought. Then it came to him.

Garlic!

Vampires hate garlic. If he could trick his parents into eating a lot of garlic, it would stop them from being vampires.

Kevin found just the right dish for them. Chicken stuffed with garlic butter.

< 23 >

It was quite a shock for Kevin's mom when he told her he wanted to cook them dinner.

"You can't even make toast," she said.

"You just wait and see," Kevin said. "And stay out of the kitchen."

Kevin got to work. He wanted the meal to stop his parents from being vampires for the rest of their lives.

< 24 >

He put an awful lot of garlic in the chicken. He was thrilled! He was sure this was going to work.

Kevin set the table and then called for his parents.

"It smells different," said Dad. "What is it?"

"Try it and see," said Kevin.

Kevin's mom and dad stuffed some chicken into their mouths. Dad began to choke. He fell off his chair. He knocked his whole plate of chicken and sent it zooming out of the window.

At the same time, Kevin's mom started to look crazed. Her eyes grew as big as plates. She jumped up from her chair and began to hop from one foot to the other.

< 25 >

Then she rushed to the bathroom and threw herself in the shower with all her clothes on. She stood there with her mouth open, gulping down cold water.

Kevin grabbed a jug of water and tipped it down Dad's throat.

Kevin's parents spent the next day in bed. He was banned from cooking anything ever again.

Kevin didn't mind the kitchen ban. But his problem had not gone away. How could he stop his parents from being vampires in time for the dance?

If he didn't go to the dance, he knew who would dance with Miranda. Grant, of course.

< 26 >

< 27 >

< 28 >

CHAPTER 4

BIG FEET
BIG TROUBLE

Grant was very good-looking and very tall. He was also very full of himself, and he was a bully.

Kevin hated Grant.

Grant hated Kevin.

Kevin stayed away from Grant because Grant had long arms with fists and long legs with boots.

< 29 >

For some reason, Miranda seemed to like Grant. Kevin didn't know why. It was very annoying.

Besides that, what was he going to do about his parents who were still Grade Three Vampires?

Kevin went to the school library to see what he could find out about vampires and vampire cures.

< 30 >

There was only one book about vampires, and it was full of stupid jokes.

Just then, Miranda came into the library. Kevin almost fell off his chair. He looked around. He was alone with Miranda! At last, he could talk to her about the dance!

Miranda saw Kevin and walked over to him. She stood so close that Kevin could hear her breathing.

She just looked at him. She didn't smile. She never smiled. He would love to make her smile.

He stared up at her.

"Why are you reading a book about vampires?" she asked.

"I don't know. It was just sitting here."

Miranda nodded.

< 31 >

There was a long silence.

I have to stop staring at her, Kevin
thought. I have to say something.

< 32 >

Kevin looked at Miranda's feet. She was wearing a pair of pink sneakers.

What could he say? He must say something to her.

"What size shoes do you wear?" he asked her.

As soon as he said it, Kevin thought, I am the biggest dumbo in all of dumbo land.

Miranda grabbed the vampire book and hit him with it.

Bop!

"Are you saying I've got big feet? You are so rude!" said Miranda.

Blapp!

Miranda hit him again and rushed out of the library.

< 33 >

Kevin just sat there. How could he have been so stupid? Why didn't he ask her to the dance with him? Why did he say anything about her shoe size?

He was just putting the vampire book back when he saw another book on the shelf.

All About Hypnosis.

< 34 >

CHAPTER 5

LOOK INTO MY EYES

Kevin started to read the book on hypnosis. The more he read, the more excited he got. The author said that hypnosis could be used to stop people from smoking or snoring or eating too much. You could use hypnosis to make people do what you wanted.

Kevin decided he could use hypnosis to stop his parents from being vampires. All he had to do was to put them into a dream state.

< 35 >

Kevin would need to swing something from side to side in front of his parents' faces. They would stare at it and would slowly slip into a dream state. Then he could tell them to do just what he wanted. Great!

As soon as he got home that afternoon, Kevin got out his yo-yo and tried it out in front of the mirror. He swung it from side to side. He stared at it. He spoke softly to himself.

"You are feeling very sleepy, you are feeling sleepy."

Bang!

He fell asleep and crashed to the floor. It worked! All he had to do now was try the same trick on his parents and hypnotize them.

< 36 >

His mom and dad were sitting in the living room, watching TV. Kevin walked in and smiled at them. "Can I show you a trick with my yo-yo?" he said.

"Will it take long?" said his mom. She didn't want to miss a minute of her TV show.

"No. It's very quick," Kevin told her.

Kevin sat his parents close to each other and swung the yo-yo from side to side in front of them.

"Keep looking at it," he began in a soft voice.

The yo-yo went from side to side.

Mom's and Dad's eyes went from side to side, too. Their heads began to nod sleepily.

< 37 >

< 38 >

"You're feeling sleepy," Kevin said. "You can't keep your eyes open. You are asleep, asleep, in a very deep sleep."

Mom began to snore. Soon both his parents were leaning against each other, fast asleep.

Kevin went on. "You will never want to suck blood again. You will stop being vampires. You will be nice, normal people."

He stopped and looked at his parents. They were asleep and snoring. Things were looking good.

"Raise your right arm," said Kevin.

They both slowly raised their arms.

His parents were in his power! He could make them do anything!

< 39 >

"Dad, stick your finger in Mom's ear. Now, Mom, stick your finger up Dad's nose."

Kevin was laughing so much he couldn't go on.

He knew that the hypnosis was working.

"I will count up to three, and you will both wake up. You will not remember anything. One, two, three!"

< 40 >

"What's been going on?" asked his dad as he woke up.

"I was showing you a trick with my yo-yo," Kevin said with a grin.

And that was that. All Kevin had to do was sit back and wait and see.

Were his parents finally cured of being vampires?

< 41 >

CHAPTER 6

THE LETTER

Three days went by, and Kevin's parents didn't bite anyone. It was great. He no longer had to live with vampire parents!

He could safely go to the dance and so could everyone else. All he had to do now was see if he could get Miranda to dance with him. Maybe she would, if he said he was sorry he asked about her shoe size.

< 42 >

There was only one day to go, so Kevin didn't have much time. The problem was that Miranda always had a huge crowd of boys around her. And Grant was always nearby.

Kevin could never see her alone.

Kevin made up his mind that he would write her a letter. He worked on it during Math class. He had to get it just right.

"Kevin? Kevin? Are you with us Kevin? Is there anyone there? Kevin?" It was Mrs. Fottle. She was standing next to him, gazing down.

She shook her head. "You were dreaming again," said Mrs. Fottle.

< 43 >

"I was going to ask if you could tell us what a triangle is called if its three sides are the same length," she added. "But I can see that you are doing something far more important. Let's see what you've been writing. No, don't try to hide it. I want to have a look. Thank you."

Mrs. Fottle picked up the letter. She began to read it out loud. "I didn't mean to say that you have big feet."

The rest of the class began to laugh.

Mrs. Fottle read on. "I think you have the most beautiful feet in the whole world."

< 44 >

The class exploded. Some kids were holding their sides they were laughing so much. "I would die to have feet like yours," she read.

< 45 >

Now half the class was rolling on the floor.

Mrs. Fottle put the note back on Kevin's desk.

"Well," she began. "I wonder who this note is for. Kevin, would you like to tell us?"

Kevin wanted to die. How could he tell everyone in the class that it was for Miranda? She was staring hard at him. Kevin knew that if he said the letter was for her, she would never speak to him again.

Kevin looked up at his teacher. "It's for you, Mrs. Fottle."

All of his classmates stopped laughing and stared at Kevin with their mouths hanging open.

< 46 >

Mrs. Fottle knew the letter wasn't for her. But what she did next was something that Kevin would always remember.

"It's a private letter," she said. "I'm very sorry, Kevin. I should never have read it out loud."

She meant it. The class stopped laughing. Mrs. Fottle went back to her desk and sat down. She began to talk about Math again.

Kevin couldn't finish his letter after that. He knew he would never be able to speak to Miranda now. His whole life was a mess.

As soon as he got home, Kevin went up to his room and threw himself down on his bed.

< 47 >

He had stopped his parents from being vampires, but the one thing he wanted most would never happen.

However, when Kevin opened up his backpack, he found a note.

Dear Kevin,

Those were such sweet things to say about my feet. I would like to dance with you tomorrow night. See you there!

Love,

Miranda xxx

Kevin read the letter that night at least fifty times.

< 48 >

CHAPTER 7

THE SCHOOL DANCE

When Kevin walked into the school gym on the night of the dance, he knew it was a night he would always remember. His mom and dad hadn't done anything a vampire would do for over a week. Kevin was sure that the hypnosis had worked. His parents would never suck blood again.

The hall looked fantastic. The dance was in full swing. Music was pounding.

< 49 >

< 50 >

Kevin looked around in the dim light for Miranda.

"Come and dance!" someone said behind him.

Kevin turned around. It was Mom. She grabbed him and began to twist and turn. Kevin could have died with shame. He prayed that Miranda wouldn't see him!

Then he saw Miranda just for a moment. She was sitting on the far side of the gym. She looked like an angel, but an angel with a frown. Kevin wanted to make her smile.

Boys gathered all around her, but she wasn't getting up to dance. Grant was standing beside her, but she wasn't even looking at him.

< 51 >

Kevin smiled. He had Miranda's note in his pocket. He knew Miranda was waiting for him. Soon he would be dancing with her. He began to make his way across the room.

"Kevin! Come and dance. Tell me you've forgiven me." This time it was Mrs. Fottle.

This night was like a very bad dream! First his mom and now his teacher!

"I can't dance with you," began Kevin, but Mrs. Fottle pulled him to her chest and spun him around until he was dizzy.

"You're a great dancer," she said.

"I've got to go now," Kevin said.

"Thank you for the dance," he added politely.

< 52 >

He rushed off. Where was Miranda? She was gone, and the boys around her were gone, too. Kevin's heart began to pound. He couldn't lose her now!

Then the screaming began.

Scared boys and girls were rushing around, yelling. Parents and teachers hung on to each other for safety.

But why?

Oh, no! Kevin saw the first zombie. It was Grant. He awkwardly walked through the hall with his arms held out in front of him. His face was white, and his eyes rolled up inside his head. He looked revolting.

Kevin looked at Grant's neck. Yes! He could see two fang-holes.

Kevin's heart sank into his boots.

< 53 >

< 54 >

< 55 >

The hypnosis had worn off. His parents had gone back to being vampires again.

Behind Grant stood another zombie, and another, and another! There were zombies everywhere. They were stomping through the hall, and all around them people yelled and waved their arms about and fainted, landing in great big heaps.

Behind the zombies, Kevin could see his parents. They hadn't had any fresh blood for two weeks, and now they had an entire pile of people to choose from. This was the disaster he had been trying to stop all along.

Then Kevin had an awful thought. Miranda was in danger!

< 56 >

She was still frowning, and she was standing right next to his parents. He had to save her!

Kevin dashed across the hall. He pushed through the zombies.

He rushed past his parents and grabbed Miranda.

"This way!" he shouted. "I'll save you! I'll get you out of here! Come on!"

Kevin and Miranda ran to the gym door. "Don't let go of my hand! Come on, this way. We'll be safe down here!"

They ran down a dark hallway. Kevin threw open the library door.

They stopped panting. Miranda was standing right next to Kevin. He could almost hear her heart beat.

< 57 >

She was still gripping his hand.

Kevin wanted this moment to last forever. At last, he was alone at last with Miranda! She gazed at him.

"You are so brave, Kevin," she said.

He turned and looked at her. She smiled at him.

That was when Kevin realized it wasn't his parents who had caused the disaster at the dance.

Miranda had fangs.

She was a vampire!

Too bad he left his yo-yo at home.

< 58 >

< 59 >

ABOUT THE AUTHOR

Jeremy Strong enjoys writing funny books for children. He says that he loves to make people smile and laugh. He has even had one of his books made into a TV show.

Jeremy travels throughout England and Europe talking to kids at schools and libraries. Jeremy lives in Somerset, England, United Kingdom, with his wife and cats.

ABOUT THE ILLUSTRATOR

Scoular Anderson was born in Scotland and attended the Art School in Glasgow. His first name is actually Tom, but when he was a year old his mother decided she didn't like that name so she started calling him by his middle name instead. "Scoular" was actually the last name of his great and great-great grandparents. Scoular once worked at a newspaper stand, and as an art teacher where he taught students not to stick paintbrushes down the sink drain.

GLOSSARY

crazed (KRAZD)—frightened, confused

heap (HEEP)—a pile, such as a pile of dirty clothes on the floor

hypnosis (hip-NO-sis)—the process of putting someone into a trance, or a sleeplike state

revolting (ri-VOHLT-ing)—disgusting

shame (SHAME)—feeling bad or embarrassed about something

zombie (ZOM-bee)—a dead body that moves, or a living being who is under the control of another person

Discussion Questions

1. Why does it bother Kevin that he's the only one in his family who's not a vampire?

2. What clues does the author give that Miranda might not be an ordinary girl?

3. Even though Kevin's parents are vampires, his family is like many other families. What kinds of problems does Kevin have with his parents? How does Kevin feel about his parents attending the school dance and why?

WRITING PROMPTS

1. Kevin tried to rid his parents of their vampire tendencies by using garlic. Describe some other things Kevin might have done to keep his parents from acting like vampires.

2. When Kevin got home from school one day, he found a note from Miranda in his backpack. Pretend that you found a note that someone left for you. It has some really good news. What does the letter say?

3. Kevin doesn't like Grant, mostly because both he and Grant are competing for Miranda's attention. Most likely, Kevin is jealous. Write about a time when you were jealous of someone in your class. What caused you to feel jealous? How did you handle your jealousy?

INTERNET SITES

Do you want to know more about subjects related to this book? Or are you interested in learning about other topics? Then check out FactHound, a fun, easy way to find Internet sites.

Our investigative staff has already sniffed out great sites for you!

Here's how to use FactHound:

1. Visit *www.facthound.com*

2. Select your grade level.

3. To learn more about subjects related to this book, type in the book's ISBN number: **1598891049**.

4. Click the **Fetch It** button.

FactHound will fetch the best Internet sites for you!